I0648815

Edward L. Blanchard

Jack in the Box; or, Harlequin, Little Tom Tucker and the

Three wise men of Gotham.

Grand comic Christmas pantomime

Edward L. Blanchard

Jack in the Box; or, Harlequin, Little Tom Tucker and the Three wise men of Gotham.
Grand comic Christmas pantomime

ISBN/EAN: 9783337024864

Printed in Europe, USA, Canada, Australia, Japan

Cover: Foto ©Andreas Hilbeck / pixelio.de

More available books at **www.hansebooks.com**

THEATRE  ROYAL

DRURY LANE.

Sole Lessee and Manager - Mr. F. B. CHATTERTON.

JACK IN THE BOX;

OR,

HARLEQUIN LITTLE TOM TUCKER,

AND

THE THREE WISE MEN OF GOTHAM.

GRAND COMIC CHRISTMAS PANTOMIME.

BY

E. L. BLANCHARD,

Author of " Hop o' my Thumb," "Sinbad the Sailor," "Little Goody Two Shoes," "House that Jack Built," "Robin Hood," "Little King Pippin," "Jack the Giant Killer," "Puss in Boots," "Beauty and the Beast," "Peter Wilkins," "Little Jack Horner," "King Humming Top," "Harlequin Hudibras," "Margery Daw," "Seven Ages of Man," "Dragon of Wantley," "Tom Thumb the Great," "The Children in the Wood," &c., &c., &c.

LONDON :

TUCK & CO., 6, UNION COURT, OLD BROAD STREET.

1873.

PRICE SIXPENCE.

JACK IN THE BOX;

OR,

HARLEQUIN LITTLE TOM TUCKER

AND

THE THREE WISE MEN OF GOTHAM.

GRAND COMIC CHRISTMAS PANTOMIME.

BY

E. L. BLANCHARD,

Author of " Hop o' my Thumb," " Sinbad the Sailor," " Little Goody Two Shoes," " House that Jack Built," " Robin Hood," " Little King Pippin," " Jack the Giant Killer," " Puss in Boots," " Beauty and the Beast," " Peter Wilkins," " Little Jack Horner," " King Humming Top," " Harlequin Hudibras," " Margery Daw," " Seven Ages of Man," " Dragon of Wantley," " Tom Thumb the Great," " The Children in the Wood," &c., &c., &c.

LONDON:

TUCK & CO., 6, UNION COURT, OLD BROAD STREET, E.C.

1873.

THEATRE ROYAL DRURY LANE.

THIS EVENING, THE DRURY LANE NEW GRAND CHRISTMAS
COMIC ANNUAL,

Illustrative of old English Folk-Lore and Nursery Legends, entitled

JACK IN THE BOX;

OR, HARLEQUIN

LITTLE TOM TUCKER & THE THREE MEN OF GOTHAM.

" Three wise men of Gotham went to sea in a bowl.   Had the bowl been
stronger our story would have been longer."—*Ancient Legend of the Nursery.*

The Scenery and Effects entirely new, by
MR. WILLIAM BEVERLY,
Whose personal services are exclusively devoted to illustrating the productions
at this theatre; assisted by
MESSRS. ROBSON, PETFORD, YARNOLD, & CUTHBERT.
The Overture, Airs de Ballet, and Songs, composed and arranged by
MR. W. C. LEVEY.
The characteristic Costumes designed by
OLIVER OLDSTYLE.
The Properties, Tricks, Changes, and Transformations, by
MR. A. J. BRADWELL AND ASSISTANTS.
The Costumes by MRS. LAWLER and MR. VOKES.
The Machinery by MR. J. TUCKER.
The Gas Illuminations by MR. J. HINCKLEY.
The Scenes of the Harlequinade by
MESSRS. CORMACK, F. EVANS, & HARVEY.
The grotesque Extravaganza by
E. L. BLANCHARD,
Author of all the Drury Lane Annuals successively produced here for twenty-
four years.
The Ballets arranged and the Pantomime produced by
MR. JOHN CORMACK,
Under the personal supervision of the Author and
MR. F. B. CHATTERTON.

Synopsis of Scenery, Incidents, and Characters.

THE

VILLAGE OF GOTHAM BY SUNSET,

WITH SAW-MILL, BROOK, & TIMBER YARD.

Ralph Roysterdoyster		
Richard Higgledypiggledy	The Three Wise Men of Gotham	MR. HOGAN. MR. NAYLOR. MR. LICKFOLD.
Robin de Bobbin		

Villagers of Gotham—Messrs. Willy, Nilly, Silly, Noodle, Numskull, Nincompoop, &c.   Cuckoo—Master Twonotes.

Prince Felix, of the Fortunate Isles (disguised as
Tom Tucker, a travelling Artisan)   ...   MISS HARRIET COVENEY.

Cockalorum the Great, King of Cockaigne ...   MR. BRITTAIN WRIGHT.

"In the Land of Cockaigne, fowls, ready roasted, cry 'Come, eat me!' and roasted geese fly into the house, exclaiming 'All hot! all hot!'"—*Old Story.*

The Princess Poppet ... (his daughter) ... MISS ALMA MURRAY.

Grand Chamberlain   ...   . MR. BIGWIG.

Court Physician   ...   .   MR. GOLDNOB.

Lord High Treasurer   ...   . MR. PURSY.

Chief Justice   ...   .   MR. WISYWERSEY.

Chancellor of Exchequer ...   . MR. CHINKS.

President of Council   ...   . MR. WINKS.

Master of the Horse   ...   . MR. BLINKS.

Courtiers—Messrs. Bob, Bowdown and Nodaway.   Guards—Messrs. Stiff, Starch, Shoulderarms, Izewright, and Standatease.   Nurse—Mrs. Caudle. Ladies-in-Waiting—Mesdames Flitter, Flutter, Simper, Whimper, Ogle, and Flirtaway.

How the Wise Men of Gotham go to sea in a bowl, and how the strange story is told of the gathering of the Fairies on the Village Common once every hundred years.

MUSHROOM COMMON.

ON MIDSUMMER EVE.

Elfina   ...   (Queen of the Fairies)   ...   MISS SYLVIA HODSON.

How the mushrooms spring up at the midnight hour, and how the adventurous Prince meets with some awfully jolly fun-gus, and is allowed to witness

THE FAIRIES' FANCY FAIR

AND FLOWER SHOW.

" Oh, take me on your knee, mother, and listen, mother of mine :
   A hundred fairies danced last night, and the harpers they were nine.
   'Twas merry the sound of the harpstrings, and their dancing feet so small,
   But, oh, the tales they had to tell were merrier far than all."

Harmonia   ...   (presiding Fairy at the Music Stall)   ...   MISS RUSSELL.

With a new Song "The Fairies' Fancy Fair," written by E. L. Blanchard, composed by W. C. Levey, and published by Duff & Stewart, 147, Oxford Street.

Jack in the Box   ...   .   MR. F. EVANS.
Fairy Cornucopia   ...   .   MISS MOWBRAY.
Attendant Fairies—MISSES MILLER, A. HAMILTON, D'ARCY, L. GROSVENOR, FITZJAMES, LOUISE BRUNTON, HELEN TEMPLE, and BEAUMONT.

GRAND BALLET BY ONE HUNDRED CORYPHEES.
Principal Danseuses   ...   MADDLES. A. GEDDA and TRAVAILLE.

THE

CABINET of KING COCKALORUM.

Maid of Honour—Miss Clara Jecks.   Herald—Mr. Hullah Bellew.

The wonderful appearance and disappearance of Jack-in-the-Box, and what followed thereupon.

COURT OF THE KING OF COCKAIGNE.

The Toy—the Talisman and the Touch—an extraordinary Sum in Reduction, and the Proof in Small Figures.

" And so we must all be small, dear boys,
   And so we must all be small,
   Till we our great faults can recall, dear boys,
   We must be all of us small."

BUTTERCUP GREEN

ON NURSERY ISLAND.

" Little Bo-Peep has lost her sheep, and cannot tell where to find them,
Leave them alone and they'll come home, and bring their tails behind them."

Little Tom Tucker ... ... MISS AMALIA.

Little Bo-Peep ... ... MISS VIOLET CAMERON.

Jack Horner, Peter Piper, Patacake Baker's Man, Margery Daw, Mr. and
Mrs. Jack Sprat, Humpty Dumpty, Simple Simon, Little Boy Blue, Little
Miss Muffet, and other residents in Nursery Island, by a host of Juvenile
Auxiliaries.

A CHILDREN'S BALLET OF BUTTERCUPS & DAISIES.

THE

BROKEN BOWL ON THE BLACK ROCKS.

How the Three Wise Men of Gotham find their voyage terminated, and
how the earth-imprisoned Fairy is liberated by the proceeds of the
Fairies' Fancy Fair.

Goblina ... (the dark Fairy) ... MISS KATE VAUGHAN.

The Reformation, Restoration, Reconciliation, and Transformation.

THE GOLDEN LAND OF PLENTY

AND

HARVEST HOME OF THE FAIRIES.

The Fairy Cornucopia ... ... MISS MOWBRAY.

" To scatter plenty o'er a smiling land,
And read their history in a nation's eyes."—*Gray.*

GRAND TRANSFORMATION!

OLDRIDGE'S
BALM OF COLUMBIA.

WHY DOES HAIR FALL OFF?

For many causes. Sometimes from local disturbing agencies, such as sickness; sometimes from neglect in cleansing; but most frequently from decay in the saps and tissues which supply each individual hair.

In each case **OLDRIDGE'S BALM OF COLUMBIA** is an excellent corrective of the many insidious sources of decay
WHICH RUINS NATURE'S CHIEF ORNAMENT.
It stimulates, strengthens, and increases the growth of Hair; softens and nourishes it when grown; arrests its decline, and cleanses from dandruff. Besides this, it acts on those pigments the constant supply of which is essential to the hair retaining its colour.

THE HAIR OF THE HEAD,
AND THE
WHISKERS AND MUSTACHIOS.
Are alike benefited. If used in childhood it forms the basis of a magnificent head of Hair, prevents Baldness in mature age, and obviates the use of dyes and poisonous restoratives.

ESTABLISHED SIXTY YEARS
(A sufficient guarantee of its efficacy).
Sold by all Perfumers and Chemists, at 3s. 6d., 6s., and 11s. only. Wholesale and Retail by the Proprietors.

C. & A. OLDRIDGE,
22, WELLINGTON STREET, STRAND,
LONDON, W.C.

THE WISE MEN OF GOTHAM.

THE Village of Gotham, so renowned in story, is seven miles from Nottingham. In the Domesday Survey the village is said to be called Gotham from goats, which being much cherished here, it was called Goat's Home, or dwelling. It is, even now, frequently pronounced Gote-ham. Warton, speaking of the " idle pranks of the men of Gotham," observes, " that such pranks bore a reference to some customary law tenures belonging to that place or its neighbourhood, now grown obsolete." Hearne also says, " Nor is there more reason to esteem the merry tales of the mad-men of Gotham (which was much valued and cried up in the time of Henry VIII., though now sold at ballad-singers' stalls) as alto-gether a romance : a certain skilful person having told me, more than once, that they formerly held lands there by such sports and customs as are touched upon in this book." Fuller says, that the proverb " ' As wise as a man of Gotham,' passeth publicly for the paraphrasis of a fool ; and a hundred fopperies are forged and fathered on the townsfolk of Gotham." It has been observed, however, that a custom prevailed, even amongst the earliest nations, as stigmatising some particular spot as remarkable for stupidity. Thus, amongst the Asiatics, Phrygia was considered as the Gotham of that day ; Abdera, amongst the Thracians ; and Bœotia among the Greeks. It is evident that considerable publicity had been given to the many ridiculous fables, traditionally told, of the men of Gotham ; particularly of their having often heard the cuckoo, but never having seen her, and therefore hedged in a bush whence her note seemed to proceed, that, being confined within so small a compass, they might at length catch her and satisfy their curiosity. What gave rise to the story is not now remembered, but there is, at a place called Courthill, in this parish, a bush still designated by the name of the " Cuckoo bush." The present inhabitants, how-ever, turn this hill to a better purpose than their ancestors did, as they work on the side of it two very fine quarries ; one of gypsum, in large blocks ; the other of a reddish stone, sufficiently hard for building, but calcareous, and fit either to burn into lime, or to polish as marble. The book alluded to by Hearne, is mentioned by Walpole, who says : "'The Merry Tales of the Mad Men of Gotham,' a book extremely admired, and often reprinted in that age, was written by Lucas de Heere, a Flemish painter who resided in England in the time of Elizabeth." Wood, however, is of a different opinion, and tells us that the tales were written by one Andrew Borde, or Andreas Perforatus as he calls himself. This facetious gentleman was a kind of travelling quack ; and it is sup-posed that the name and occupation of a Merry Andrew took its rise from him.   There is an old black letter edition of the work at the Bodleian Library at Oxford, called "Certaine Merry Tales of the Mad Men of Gotham, compiled in the reign of Henry VIII., by Andrew Borde, an eminent physician of that period."   One of these stories is related nearly in the following words :—

"There were two men of Gotham, and the one of them was going to the market of Nottingham to buy sheepe, and the other came from the market ; and both met together upon Nottingham bridge. 'Well met,' said the one to the other.   'Whither bee ye going ?' said he that came from Nottingham.' 'Marry,' said he that was going thither, 'I go to that market to buy sheepe.' 'Buy sheepe !' said the other, 'and which way wilt thou bring them home ?' 'Marry,' said the other, 'I will bring them over this bridge.'   'By Robin Hood,' said he that came from Notting-ham, 'but thou shalt not.'   'By Maid Marian,' said he that was going thitherward, 'but I will.'   'Thou shalt not,' said the one.   'I will,' said the other.   '*Ter here*,' said the one.   '*Shue there*,' said the other.   Then they beat their staves against the ground, one against the other, as there had been a hundred sheep betwixt them. 'Hold in,' said the one.   'Beware the leaping over the bridge of my sheepe,' said the other.   'They shall not come this way,' said the one. 'But they shall,' said the other. 'Then,' said the other, 'and if thou make much to do, I will put my finger in thy mouth.' 'A—thou wilt,' said the other.   And as they were at their contention, another man of Gotham came by from the market, with a sacke of meale upon his horse, and seeing and hearing his neighbours in strife about sheepe, and none betwixt them, said, 'Ah ! fooles, will you never learn wit ?' 'Help me,' said he that had the meal, 'and lay my sack upon my shoulder.' They did soe ; and he went to one side of the bridge, and unloosed the mouth of the sacke, and did shake out all his meale into the river. 'Now neighbours,' said he, 'how much meale is there in my sacke?' 'Marry! there is none at all,' said they. 'Now, by my faith,' said he, 'even as much wit is in your heads to strive for that thing you have not.' Which was the wisest of all these three persons, judge you?"

There is also a tale of two brothers, one of whom wished for as many oxen as he saw stars, whilst the other, wishing for a pasture as wide as the firmament, they quarrelled and killed each other about the pasturage of the oxen: and another of a good woman who, when left at home by her husband, with directions to wet the meal before she gave it to the pigs, threw the meal into the well, and the pigs after it. The people of Gotham have a tradition that their folly was like Edgar's madness, put on for the occasion; and Throsby relates that, according to this tradition, "'the cuckoo bush' was merely planted to commemorate a trick which the inhabitants of Gotham put upon King John, who, passing through this place towards Nottingham, and intending to go over the meadows, was prevented by the villagers, who supposed that the ground over which a king passed must ever after remain a public road. The king, incensed at their proceedings, sent from his court soon after some of his officers to inquire of them the reason of their incivility and ill-treatment, in order that he might duly apportion the punishment, by way of fine, &c. The Gothamites, hearing of their approach, thought of an expedient to turn away his displeasure; for when the messengers arrived, they found some of the inhabitants endeavouring to drown an eel in a pool of water; some employed in dragging carts upon a large barn, in order to shade the wood from the sun; others were tumbling their cheeses down hill, that they might find their way to Nottingham market for sale; and some employed in hedging in a cuckoo, which had perched upon an old bush that stood where the present one now stands— in short, they were all occupied in some foolish way or other, which convinced the King's officers that they were a village of fools!"

THE ANNUAL RECEIPTS

OF THE

BIRKBECK BUILDING SOCIETY

EXCEED THREE MILLIONS!

HOW TO PURCHASE A HOUSE

For Two Guineas per Month, with Immediate Possession and no Rent to Pay. Apply at the Office of the

BIRKBECK BUILDING SOCIETY,

29 & 30, SOUTHAMPTON BUILDINGS, CHANCERY LANE.

HOW TO PURCHASE A PLOT OF LAND

For Five Shillings per Month, with Immediate Possession, either for Building or Gardening Purposes. Apply at the Office of the

BIRKBECK FREEHOLD LAND SOCIETY,

29 & 30, SOUTHAMPTON BUILDINGS, CHANCERY LANE.

HOW TO INVEST YOUR MONEY

With safety, at £4 per cent. Interest. Apply at the Office of the

BIRKBECK BANK.

All sums under £50 payable upon demand. Current accounts opened similar to ordinary Bankers. Cheque-books supplied.

Office hours from 10 till 4, on Mondays from 10 till 9, and on Saturdays from 10 till 2 o'clock.

A small Pamphlet, containing full particulars, may be obtained Gratis, or sent post free on application to

FRANCIS RAVENSCROFT, *Manager.*

JACK IN THE BOX.

View of the Village of Gotham—Sunset—with Saw Mill, Brook, and Timber Yard.

Music. The THREE WISE MEN *and all the* VILLAGERS *of Gotham discovered busily looking for Needles in Bundles of Hay, as curtain rises to symphony of opening chorus.*

Air—Old English—" The Maypole."

We've searched about, but can't find out
    The place where they can be ;
Tho' in and out, and round about
    That place we've tried to see.
They should be somewhere here,
    And ought to be, we say ;
But we've stumbled, grumbled, mumbled, fumbled,
    Tumbled about the hay.
Tumbled, fumbled, mumbled, grumbled,
    Stumbled about the hay.

RALPH.   Well, have you got 'em ?

RICHARD.   Got 'em ? we can't find 'em.
    These bundles must have left them all behind them.

ROBIN.   Looking for needles here we've been all day.

RALPH.   Yet that's the place to look for them, folks say.

ROBIN.   Well, possibly a bowl requires no stitching.

RICHARD. Sagacious thought! that notion is bewitching.
        Better the planks should pasted be together,
        Then they will bid defiance to the weather.

RALPH.   We have been called, by men of every nation,
        The greatest set of boobies in creation;
        But after this, a question will arise
        Whether the men of Gotham are not wise.

ROBIN.   A few tin tacks would not be a bad plan;
        We'll nail the planks together, if we can.

RALPH.   Tin tacks! the very thing, I have no doubt.
        Haven't you heard that ships take tacks about?

RICHARD.   At all events, we three are on the whole
        All bent on going to sea.

RALPH.
  and   And in a bowl.
ROBIN.

RALPH.   Then for provision, stores we must lay in—
                                (*Note of Cuckoo.*)
        Hark! there's a cuckoo!   Let us hedge him in.

(*Music. As the Cuckoo hops on with his familiar note,* ROBIN,
    RALPH, *and* RICHARD, *with the rest of the Men of Gotham, hide
    each behind a Bundle of Hay—gradually hopping down, they
    enclose the Cuckoo, leaving him however visible to audience.*)

RALPH.   This is a clever notion, I must say—
        We have him safe.
                    (*Cuckoo goes over their heads and Exits.*)

OMNES.   Look! See! He flies away!

(*Quick music.   Fruitless chase of Villagers, who fling off their
    Bundles of Hay after Cuckoo.*)

                (ROBIN *brings on three cheeses.*)

ROBIN.   Here are three cheeses.

RICHARD.   Cheeses! we want meat.

RALPH.   Of course, we beef and mutton ought to eat.

Send them to market. they will sell themselves ;
And what they bring we'll place upon our shelves.
RICHARD. There, roll them down the hill.   They know the way,-
RALPH. And fetch good prices, for it's market day.

(The three Cheeses are rolled off, P. S.)

ROBIN. I wish I'd sheep as there are stars on high.
RICHARD. And I a field as big as the whole sky.
You shouldn't graze your sheep, tho', in my field.
ROBIN. Oh ! wouldn't I.
RICHARD.   No—that point I'd never yield.
ROBIN. Then, let this teach thee that I would and will.
RALPH. Forbear ! A stranger's coming up the hill,—
Of noble presence, tho' in humble guise,
He may assist us—he looks very wise.

*(Music. Enter with bundle over his shoulder, PRINCE FELIX of the
Fortunate Isles, disguised as TOM TUCKER, a travelling artisan.)*

PRINCE. Ah ! gentlemen of Gotham.   Hail—good day—
Will fair day's work secure a fair day's pay ?
I am a travelling workman, and can take
A share in anything you want to make.
RALPH. The very man ; we're going to build a bowl.
PRINCE. Then I'll assist you with my heart and soul.
RICHARD. It's a big bowl, we are all here going to sea in it?
PRINCE. I see, it must have room enough for three in it.
RALPH. Wonderful man !—I said how wise he looked.
PRINCE. Hammer, and wood, and nails,—that job is booked.
ROBIN. He knows at once the very things to get.
RICHARD. I've never seen a workman like him yet.
PRINCE *(aside)*. They little know a prince is here before 'em,.
Who loves the daughter of King Cockalorum ;
Her picture put my heart in quite a pucker.
RALPH. Your name is—
PRINCE.   Tom, my other name is Tucker.
Enough for dinner, work will always bring for it.

RALPH. }
RICHARD. }   And how do you get your supper?
ROBIN. }
PRINCE.   Bless you—sing for it.

Song.—PRINCE.—" *Sedition Rondo*," *Mdme. Angot.*

   I'm one who takes the world about me
     Quite as it comes, with rose or thorn ;
   Of course, it might do well without me,
     Just as it did 'ere I was born.
   But, if in lives of honest labour,
     All men do their best, I'm sure
   Every man must do good to his neighbour,
     Till all are better off than before.   (*Refrain*).
   Often with work to be done in a hurry,
   Princes and monarchs have plenty of worry,
   So I've very often thought,
   E'en honours may be dearly bought.

RALPH.   Quite my opinion, Mr. Thomas Tucker.
RICHARD. You're just in time to come to our succour.
ROBIN.   Here is our workshop, will it please you view it?
RALPH.   You make the bowl, and we'll all see you do it.
PRINCE.   You have a brook that turns a mill, however.
RALPH.   Wheels, turned by water !—Isn't water clever?
PRINCE.   Well, come along, such work I understand,
      And I'll soon turn this big bowl out of hand.

(*Music. Three men take* PRINCE *into workshop. Change of Music
" Laird of Cockpen," heard first softly as in the distance, then
approaches nearer. Villagers coming forward and intimating their
delight at the advance of the* KING *and Court*).

(*Enter* COCKALORUM *the Great, King of Cockaigne, attended by
Grand Chamberlain, Court Physician, Lord High Treasurer,
Chief Justice, Chancellor of Exchequer, President of Council,
Master of the Horse, Guards and Courtiers, &c. &c. The* PRINCESS

POPPET, *of Cockaigne, attended by Nurse, Ladies in Waiting, and her retinue).*

KING.   Here will we on our royal progress rest,
          And take refreshment as it seemeth best.
          Now, rustics, since we've visited this spot,
          We'll honour you by taking all you've got.
          Your choicest wine our royal hearts will cheer,
          While others may regale themselves on beer.

(Villagers refresh the Monarch with a flagon of wine, and distribute jugs of beer to attendants.

KING.   My temper's bad, the slightest things upset it,
          I want my way in everything, and get it.
          There's not a man in all my wide dominions,
          About my meaning can have two opinions.
          Or if he does, and daringly confesses it,
          He rues the very moment he expresses it.

(Consternation of Villagers and Courtiers.)

PRINCESS. Oh ! what a stupid place.
KING.   It is, my dear ;
          That was the reason why I brought you here.
          Now don't you think it is a pity, rather,
          My handsome child—how very like your father !—
          You should be—well, I'll mildly say " A dunce."
PRINCESS. You might have said a fool, papa, at once,
          You know I'm so like you.
KING.   In face; for t'other
          I trace a strong resemblance to your mother.
PRINCESS. That I am somewhat stupid, I admit,
          I try to learn, but can't improve a bit.
KING.   Can't you contrive to look a little wise ?
          Just shut your mouth, and open wide your eyes,
          And something nice I think that I could send you.
PRINCESS. What's that, papa?
KING.   A husband to attend you,

Who would with title give you wealth and lands,
And take a deal of trouble off my hands.
PRINCESS. What! let me have a nice new doll to play with,
        Whose arms I might pull off and make away with?
KING.   That which you wish to do, will please your lover,
        That which you can't do, leave him to discover.
        I want to hear some stupid man propose.

        (*Enter* PRINCE FELIX *from workshop*).

PRINCE. The bowl is finished, and away it goes.

                (*Bowl, with three men, seen launched.*)

        This wooden bowl, the fame of Gotham spreads,
RALPH.   We three all made it out of our own heads.
PRINCE (*aside*).   There's the princess of whom I've seen the
        picture,
        And in my heart have framed it as a fixture.
        If she requires a husband, I'm the man.
KING.   What means this bowl?
PRINCE.   To go sire where it can.
        In this big bowl three men are going to sea.
KING.   What?
PRINCE.   That's a secret sire, that rests with me.
KING.   Adventurous men, who go on the deep water,
        Proclaim that I have got a lovely daughter.
        Whoe'er with common sense that girl provides,
        Shall have her hand, my blessing, too, besides.

(*The Men of Gotham accept the commission, and bowl works off*).

PRINCE. From what I've heard, I think I know the plan.
KING.   You do! Then tell it, there's a good young man.

                THE LEGEND.

            Song.—THE PRINCE.

            Air.—" *Bay of Cherokee.*"

There's a strange old tale of the wonders to be seen
    On Midsummer eve—old style—

But your nerves must be strong, and your heart be true,
 And your conscience devoid of guile.
Every hundred years, on the neighbouring plain,
 On that night there is said to be,
If you only go there as the clock strikes twelve,
 Such a fair as we ought to see.

It's a tale you won't believe, but they tell me at the time,
 As mushrooms rise in view,
That a fair—just fancy—is held upon the green,
 By some jolly little elves and their crew.
I received the account from a very old man,
 Aged more than a century ;
He was there the very night, when it last did occur,
 And to night it again will be.

Chorus.

It's the very kind of tale to be told to the marines,
 A tale of the good old style,
Tho' our nerves may be strong, where are hearts that are true,
 With a conscience devoid of guile ?

(*The* Prince *takes the opportunity of showing his attachment to the* Princess. *The* King *interrupts their love making. The* Prince *indicates he is resolved to win the* Princess, *and be at the midnight fair. Court go off one side, and villagers the other*).

SCENE II.

Gotham Common on Midsummer Eve.

(*Enter, to Music, the* Prince, *who makes his way among the Mushrooms plentifully growing on the Common.*)

Prince. Well, here I am, the strangest of positions,
  I really think I answer all conditions.

My nerves are strong, my conscience has no sting,
And true as steel, the heart I have to bring.
I won't turn back, whate'er comes in my way;
Something advances, who are you, I say?

(*Music.   Enter the Fairy* ELFINA *disguised as Old Woman, with
  Crutch.*)

ELFINA. A poor old dame who only comes in sight,
         To gather mushrooms growing here to-night.
PRINCE. Let me assist you, ah! confound the pins.

     (*Smarting under effect of touch as he supports her arm.*)

ELFINA. Wasn't it conscience pricked you for your sins?
         Aren't you afraid, young man, whoe'er you be,
         To trust yourself here, all alone with me?
PRINCE. I know no guile, ne'er meant one any harm.
ELFINA. If so, then you're the chap to work the charm,
         Something, if you look round you circumspectly,
         Out of the common you will see directly.
         Listen! I think it is about the time.

          (*Village clock strikes twelve.*)

PRINCE. The clock strikes twelve.
ELFINA.   When ends that midnight chime
         Observe these mushrooms, what there now appears
         No one has witnessed for a hundred years.

          (*Mysterious Music.   Piano.*)

         Look there!   Behold!

                    (*Movement of Mushrooms.*)

PRINCE. The mushrooms up are springing,
         And something odd from underground are bringing.
ELFINA. You see at present everywhere among us,
         A mushroom, popularly called a fungus.
         I do but strike my crutch, and with this plunge, I
         Reveal the funny figures of the Fungi.

They get no higher wages than my thanks,
Yet here they are, with all their pretty pranks.

(ELFINA *strikes crutch, which she throws off with her disguise.*)

(*Mushrooms go through evolutions.*)

ELFINA. They have a wholesome reputation got,
Not like these toadstools, who are an awful lot.

· (*Dance of toadstools.*)

More quickly now than mushrooms here will grow,
The Fairies' Fancy Fair and Flower Show.

Rapid change to

SCENE III.

The Fairies' Fancy Fair and Flower Show.

(*Transformation of Mushrooms to the stalls at which Fairies preside. Rapid movements of the glittering elves, &c. The stage presents a general scene of animation till* ELFINA *speaks.*

ELFINA (*To* PRINCE.) Look round you; here may favoured mortals buy
Whatever article most charms the eye.
Offer no money, coin no fairies take,
With gentle words and looks the purchase make.

PRINCE. Thanks for the hint, my bargain seems a rare one,
What pretty toy will please my simple fair one?
What shall I buy for her?

(*Fairies at stalls invite custom.*)

1ST. FAIRY.   A bunch of flowers.
A choice bouquet fresh culled from beauty's bowers.

2ND. FAIRY. A feather brush removes each trace of care.
You'll find there's nothing prettier in the fair.

3RD. FAIRY.   Some rare old tapestry, quite free from fracture,
        Warranted real Goblin manufacture.
4TH. FAIRY.   Six articles entirely useless.   These
        Are most expensive, and are sure to please.
5TH. FAIRY.   Pincushions fashioned in all kinds of forms.
6TH. FAIRY.   A glass foretelling matrimonial storms.
7TH. FAIRY.   Portraits of public men who hold high places,
        A famous chance to recognise their faces.
8TH. FAIRY.   The likenesses of those, both long and deeply
        Engaged on a late trial—going cheaply.
9TH. FAIRY.   Some curious witnesses for the accused,
        No reasonable offer now refused.
PRINCE.   I have opinions not quite orthodox,
        So choose instead this simple Jack in Box.
        A more ingenious toy man ne'er devised,
        You know what's coming but are still surprised.
        Now-a-days, folks seem scarce surprised at all,
      · "Jack in the Box," I take you from the stall.

(*Music.*   PRINCE *receives from stall a Box (a large imitation of toy),
labelled "Jack in the Box," and places it on stage.*

ELFINA.   No wiser choice could mortal man have made,
        Here lies our cleverest sprite in ambuscade,
        A curious Elf, who everyone surprises.
PRINCE.   I touch the spring, then pop, and up he rises.

        Music.   Appearance of JACK IN THE BOX.)

        This is the strangest toy man ever bought.
JACK.   Want me? and Jack springs up as quick as thought.
        I'm double-jointed, light as clouds ethereal,
        And warranted well made, of best material.

(*Music.*   JACK *illustrates his elasticity by a series of movements.*)

ELFINA.   You have become his master from to-day,
        What you command, he swiftly will obey.
JACK.   Just such a faithful servant will I make you. ·
PRINCE.   You will!   Then, as your owner, off I take you.

I'll see you to a fair Princess consigned,
Of faultless form, but undeveloped mind.
About the palace you shall antics play,
She may grow wiser thro' your pranks ; away !

(*Music.*   JACK *expresses his devotion, and goes off with* PRINCE.)

ELFINA.   Last chance to-night ! what other youth appears ?
Once—only once—in every hundred years.

Song.—HARMONIA.—" *The Fairies' Fancy Fair.*"

Written by E. L. Blanchard, composed by W. C. Levey, and published by
Duff & Stewart, 147, Oxford Street.

Come, who will have this magic spell,
I have charms for every care,
Yet, not for silver fairies sell,
So buyers must beware.
Nor take we gold for what is sold,
But a look from a loving eye,
And a gentle word in the twilight heard,
Will priceless treasures buy.
Then mortals all, come round my stall,
Here no one need despair,
You get with a glance, the luckiest chance,
At the Fairies' Fancy Fair.

This Fairy charm is really cheap,
When round the neck 'tis hung,
All those who wear the locket, keep
Their hearts for ever young.
It holds you true to the one you knew,
In the brightest days of yore,
And it brings you back, by a rosy track,
To the happy old times once more.

But mortals all, at every stall,
   When hither you repair,
Hearts must not range, we have never change
   At the Fairies' Fancy Fair.

GRAND TABLEAU

AND

BALLET,

ON WHICH SCENE CHANGES TO.

SCENE IV.

The Cabinet of King Cockalorum.

(Quick Pantomime Music, and enter rapidly KING, *driving before him all his Ministers, Courtiers, &c., and followed by Guards, who range at back.)*

KING.   Don't talk to me—I'm savage, and I know it;
         When I am in a rage I let you know it.
         Groom of the Bedchamber—

                 (Trembling attendant advances.)

                 I gave you warning,
         My royal razor wasn't stropped this morning.
         Confine the caitiff fifty fathoms deep
         In lowest dungeon of the castle keep.
         Where's the First Lord in Waiting?

         (First Lord advances nervously as Groom exits.)

                 Sir, I found
         My toast this morning blacked instead of browned.

For this, until I hear of due repentance,
Twelve months in banishment shall be your sentence.
Clerk of the Kitchen—

(*Clerk advances with trembling knees.*)

Didn't I this minute
Discover gravy with a cinder in it?
This is contempt of Court—it does amaze me!
Fine him a thousand pounds, and see he pays me.

Song.—KING.

Air.—" King and Countryman."

The monarch I am of a wide domain,
I'm King of the country called Cockaigne.
I'll have my own way as long as I reign,
And after I've done I shall want it again;
As the rightful heir all, one to share all,
    Emperor of Cockaigne.

A daughter I have so dull and dense,
She hasn't the smallest grain of sense,
And the stupidest folks I found, were hence
Too wise to have her on any pretence.
As I made my rural, tour all, cure all,
    Agony of suspense.

So here I am, on my former track,
And not in the best of tempers, back;
Of suitors here if I find a lack,
I can only say there will be a whack.
Fa-laral, share all, making you care all—
    Whacketty, racketty, crack.

KING.   Where is my daughter? don't you see I'm calm?
    Where is my daugh——? you needn't feel alarm.
    Where is my daughter? Why do you not reply?
    Go off, or else your heads will by-and-by.

(*Enter* NURSE, *with Lady in Waiting.*)

    Oh ! here is one, who from her situation,
    Ought to possess a little information.
    Where's the princess, immediately away to her,
    State that her father has a word to say to her.

LADY IN WAITING.   There ! don't you hear, nurse ? Why don't
      you obey ?
    Great Cockalorum has a word to say.

(*Exit* NURSE.)

KING.   A word ! I shall want hundreds ere I've done.

(*Enter* PRINCESS POPPET.)

    Oh ! here you are, you precious simpleton !
    You know I'm anxious, girl, you should be married,
    Ere by some revolution off I'm carried.
    Such things have been and may be once again,
    If you were wedded, you might hope to reign.

PRINCESS. But I'm so stupid—I should not know how.

KING.   That's no objection, government rules now.
    You only sit, and nod, and say " All right !"
    I've reigned so many a year.

PRINCESS.   Seems easy, quite.

KING.   Of course it is, but in the wedded state,
    A man requires an intellectual mate.
    I don't expect you to have brains like Plato's,
    But you might learn to——well, say, boil potatoes.

PRINCESS. Do you believe in fairies, pa ?

KING.   No, pooh !

PRINCESS. I didn't once, but now I think I do.
    I had a dream last night, and during sleep
    They gave me such a pretty toy to keep.
    With that, my education seemed completed,
    And fairies said—

KING.   .   You're always so conceited ;

You think because you're pretty, that's enough,
You'll find it isn't.

PRINCESS.   Fairies said that——

KING.   Stuff!

I'll hear no more. As princely suitors rose up
And asked your hand, you turned your pretty nose up.
And now I've travelled the whole country thro',
No lord seems fool enough to look at you.

(Enter HERALD *with Trumpet.)*

HERALD. Sire, I'm desired—

KING.   You are, to quickly tell——

HERALD. A handsome stranger has arrived.

KING.   .   'Tis well.

Admit him to our royal presence. Stay!
What ho! B'low there, trumpets—blow away.

(Exit HERALD.*)*

(Vehement Flourish of Trumpets.)

By that, the stranger waiting for admission
Will know we are in a flourishing condition.
Now leave each syllable to your papa,
And don't reveal the silly belle you are.

(Lively Music. Enter PRINCE FELIX, *still disguised as* TOM
TUCKER, *with "Jack in the Box.")*

PRINCE. Fair lady, mighty monarch, here you see
One of good name, tho' not of high degree.

(To PRINCESS.*)*

I know you're pretty, I have heard you're proud,
Yet hope my presents here may be allowed.

PRINCESS. And you have brought——?

PRINCE *(presents Jack in Box.)*   This gift.

PRINCESS. Oh! I shall scream!
The youth and toy I pictured in my dream.

KING.   It seems a curious sort of thing.

PRINCE.   You'll say so,
      For when I touch this spring he pops away so.

(*Rapid Music. Disappearance and Reappearance of* JACK, *to the bewilderment of* KING *and Court, who vainly try to catch him.*)

PRINCE. You see this Jack in Box which I have brought,
          Is not a man that's easy to be caught.
KING.   Wonderful, really! perfect to each particle,
          What shall we say for this ingenious article?
PRINCE. Your daughter's hand.
KING.   Agreed—so let it be.
PRINCESS. This person isn't good enough for me.
          Altho' I own the toy is most complete.
PRINCE (*aside.*) 'Ere long we'll find a cure for this conceit.
  (*Aloud.*) I offer you Princess, a deep affection,
  (*Aside.*) And undertake your faults shall find correction.
  (*Aloud.*) Observe, your common toy can only squeak,
          This is a Jack who'll dance, and sing, and speak.
KING.   Capital notion; Jack with joints and jerks,
          I'll make you Chairman of our Board of Works.
PRINCE. Law Courts unbuilt would then not long remain.
JACK.   Just so—in, out, here, there, and back again.

(JACK *illustrates the swiftness of his movements by a specimen of his activity before the* KING.)

Song.—PRINCE.

Air.—"*Madame Angot.*"

Tho' humble in my calling,
    Unblemished is my name,
Let this excuse my falling
    In love with one of fame;-
Untitled tho' you take him,
    A youth of lowly life,
He dares to think you'll make him
    Well suited with a wife.

Fortune favouring,
You not wavering,
Here a husband you behold ;
Don't mind trinkets,
Don't you think it's
Bettter to have love than gold.

General Chorus.—"Fortune favouring, &c."

KING.   *Air.*—"*I should like to.*"   *Chorus only.*

I should like to.   I should like to.
I hope that she will not say "shan't."
But a bride, too, I have tried to
Long marry her off but I can't.

Duet and Chorus.   Air.—"I wish I was."

KING.

I'm not satisfied at all
With what she is, but could
I only make her something else
I very quickly would.

PRINCE.

I madly am in love,
As deep as man can be ;
But such conceit I never did meet,
As here I chance to see.

Chorus.

I wish it was to be ;
But her lips, tho' sweet as honey,
Are under a nose that turns up
At every man with money.
I wish she was again
At her school, where she should be ;
I wish she had a grain of sense,
Then she would marry me.

JACK.   *Air.—"Evans' Pantomimical."*

Peculiar thing the Princess is,
   So impudent a "cuss;"
But if you only wait awhile,
   You needn't make a fuss,
I know a plan to work a cure,
   You leave it all to us.

     Hixtum, stixtum, you shall see
     Her pride shall go down plump.
     Just touch my spring, enough for me,
     How I will make her jump!
       Oh dear! oh law! &c.
       For I am Jack in the Box!

    Chorus of others.   Repeat.

     Hixtum, stixtum, you will see
     Her pride shall go down plump.
     Just touch his spring, and quickly he
     Will make the Princess jump!
       Oh dear! oh law! &c.
       For he is Jack in the Box!

(PRINCESS *conceitedly goes off, and rest follow, dancing off to end of tune.*)

(Scene discovers)

SCENE V.

Court of the King of Cockaigne.

(All the Ministers discovered round the throne.   Enter KING, PRINCE FELIX, *Guards, &c.* KING *ascends throne with marked ceremony.)*

KING.   Here, in possession of our royal chair,
     Let Cockalorum settle this affair.

In vain to coax his child your monarch tries.
Can anybody anything advise?
As peacock proud, she's obstinate as mule.

IRISH M. Shure, don't you see what's wanted?—Its "Home Rule."
KING. Silence!
IRISH M. Home rule—it plainest common sense is.
We'll do the governing, you pay the expenses.
KING. Silence for Thomas Tucker!
PRINCE. Sire, I press
My suit as suitor to the fair Princess.
The picture of her beauty I must say
Fell short of that which I beheld to-day;
And as the fair original does exceed
All that the artist painted her, indeed
So do my feeble words but faintly show
A depth of love much more than she can know.
KING. Sensibly spoken like a good young man.
Now Thomas Tucker, if you'll find a plan
To cure her great conceit and dense stupidity,
Why you shall marry her.

(*Ministers bow assent.*)

PRINCE. Done, Sire. With rapidity
Let the Princess appear; with help of Jack
The lady to her senses I'll bring back.
KING. Call the Princess! This matter we will wind up.

(*Enter* PRINCESS, *Nurse, Ladies.*)

Now, Madam, have you made your little mind up?
PRINCESS. Not I. The fair Princess of these dominions
Has of herself the highest of opinions.
PRINCE. Then Jack in Box spring up. The name I call
Can make the greatest of them here feel small!

(JACK IN BOX *appears.*)

JACK. Behold me! The Princess, as small Bo-Peep,
Will lose her subjects, all transformed to sheep.

King of Cockaigne, Jack Horner you become;
Be a good boy and you'll pick out the plum.
Reduced in size when I one touch bestow,
Away to Nursery Island all must go.

(KING *descends throne.   Alarm of Court.*)

KING.   *Air.—" Eaton Square."   Chorus only.*

Oh ! this sort of thing is all very well,
   But I think it isn't fair ;
When you have a mind to be a swell,
   To be packed off anywhere.

PRINCE.   *Air.—" Have you seen the Shah ?   Chorus only.*

You'll see what you are boys—you'll see what you are,
   When you are sent to Nursery Land, which is peculiar.
Stuck up with pride, you would deride the wish of your Papa,
   And only answer everyone with "Psha!"

PRINCE.   *Air.—" Belle of the Ball."*

When you're small you are always delighted
   At getting some fun on the chance;
But there's nothing with which you're requited,
   In years as you come to advance.
Men remain—only bent on gain—
   And girls are bent upon beaux ;
While you all are forgetting the truths
   That from Nursery Island arose.

Chorus.

And so we must all be small, dear boys,
And so we must all be small, dear boys;
Till we our faults can recall, dear boys,
We must be all of us small.

(JACK, *during Chorus, touches each of the characters, and by the time
   the air has ended the transformation is effected. The* KING,
PRINCE, PRINCESS, *and all the Court have disappeared, and in*

their places are LITTLE BO-PEEP, *with crook,* TOM TUCKER, JACK HORNER, *with pie,* PETER PIPER, *picking his peck of pepper, Baker's Man, with cake,* MARGERY DAW, *with see-saw; and* JACK SPRATT *and* WIFE, HUMPTY DUMPTY, LITTLE MISS MUFFETT, SIMPLE SIMON, *and* LITTLE BOY BLUE, *in background.*)

TABLEAU.

(JACK IN THE BOX *points triumphantly to the result of the change he has effected, and as he goes off the characters become animated.*)

TOM T. Jack in the Box his purpose has made plain,
      We are all sent back to childhood's days again.

BO-PEEP. Where am I? Wasn't I once a great Princess?
      And isn't that my father—only less?

TOM T. Yes, that's the monarch seated in the corner.
      His kingdom is a pie, his name Jack Horner.

BO-PEEP. Our Chancellor of Exchequer—see there sticking!

TOM T. Now Peter Piper—pecks of pepper picking.

BO-PEEP. And there our Lord Chief Justice, by see-saw,
      Keeping the proper balance of the law.
      That Baker's Man, who pricks a name with holes?

TOM T. Now Pat-a-Cake, once Master of the Rolls.

BO-PEEP. My Ladies of the Court, where shall I find them?

TOM T. They're sheep, and awful tales have left behind them.

BO-PEEP. Oh, what a change! Most curious it does seem.
      When shall I hear of them?

TOM T. In Bo-Peep's dream.

(*Slow music.* TOM TUCKER *waves his hand; characters disperse, and scene changes to*)

SCENE VI.

Nursery Island.

(*Lively Pastoral Music, as scene opens.* *Enter Children gathering*

*buttercups and daisies.   Appearance of the missing sheep passing
in succession.   When they have gone off,* Bo-Peep *enters, meeting*
Tom Tucker.)

Bo-Peep. Oh, Thomas Tucker—what a lucky meeting,
   I've lost my sheep, but dreamed I heard them bleating.
   By hook or crook I'm quite resolved to find them,
Tom T. Leave them alone—no tales they'll leave behind them.
   But now no more seems Thomas Tucker chid.
Bo-Peep. I feel so different from what I did,
   No longer I'm conceited.
Tom T.   Well I never!
Bo-Peep. I've grown, too, much more sensible and clever.
   My nursery playmates with attention honour me,
   Jack Sprat has taught me lessons in economy.
   Patience from Peter Piper have I learned,
   And Simple Simon, how a penny's turned.
Tom T. While Humpty Dumpty tumbling from the wall,
   Has warned you of the danger of a fall.
Bo-Peep. Nay—I have been industrious too, you know,
   Little Miss Muffet taught me how to sew.
   And when I said at music I would try,
   Little Boy Blew his horn, and so could I.
Tom T. Why, thus endowed, you'll lead a useful life,
   And I would marry had I such a wife.
Bo-Peep. Then you shall be my little sweetheart still.
Tom T. Most charming of small mortals, so I will.
Bo-Peep. Here is my fortune—I am rich in wool,

   (*Black sheep crosses with three bags.*)

   Three bags you see, and every bag is full.
   One for Papa, once Emperor of Cockaigne,
   Two for provisions going down Red Lane.
Tom T. Why we are rich, indeed; this reformation
   Will soon make all resume their former station.

Song.—Bo-Peep.

Air.—" *Down by the Old Mill Stream.*"

If you would be contented as a farmer,
  I should be also blest.
Quite sure that you liked your little charmer,
  If only she tried to do her best.
The humblest fare, she'd gladly share,
  No frown should e'er be seen,
You'll not forget your charming little pet,
  You met upon Buttercup Green.

Refrain.

  Yes, upon Buttercup Green,
    Many happy hours shall be seen.
  Dancing every day, we'll pass the hours away,
    Living upon Buttercup Green.

(Bo-Peep's *little Fandango, and Ballet of Buttercups and Daisies.*)

(On which scene closes.)

SCENE VII.

The Broken Bowl on the Black Rocks.

(*Marked Music. Enter with their quarter staves*, Ralph, Richard, *and* Robin, *the Three Wise Men of Gotham.*)

Ralph.   Alas! we're wrecked, but had our bowl been stronger,
        No doubt our story would have been much longer.
Richard. Our voyage has been short; but still, dear brother,
        It will be long before I make another.
Robin.· Cast on these rocks, it useless is complaining,
        Let's make the best of all the staves remaining.

(*The three confer at side, while enter* (*as invisible*) *on the other side,*
  Elfina, Harmonica, *and attendants.*

C

HARMONICA. Behold, my fairy queen, here are the three
           Wise men of Gotham, who went forth to sea.
           Jack in the Box—that toy the mortal bought,
           Has to her senses Princess Poppet brought.
           And long imprisoned fays can cleave the air,
           Freed by the produce of the Fancy Fair.
RALPH. At least, if we get back to Gotham Green,.
           No one more stupid than ourselves we've seen.

(They range in line with Fairies.)

Chorus.—Air, " Conspirators' Chorus."—Madame Angot.

    When folks do wrong, which they'd better not,
    And choose to say it's a way they've got,
    The wisest course they can pursue,
    Is no such thing again to do.

ELFINA. Men talking in so sensible a strain,
           Fairies shall see you safely home again.
RALPH. Fairies!
HARMONICA.   Well, yes, that power you may perceive in us,
           It's only men of science don't believe in us.
ELFINA. Make yourselves visible to mortal eyes,
           See, who comes here arrayed in princely guise.
HARMON. The very one—How strangely things befall !—
           Who Jack in Box selected from my stall. ·

(Enter PRINCE FELIX, handsomely attired.)

PRINCE. Regaining figure, I resume my style,
           Once more Prince Felix of the Fortunate Isle.
           But where's my pretty wife who charmed my eyes,
           Improved in mind tho' much reduced in size ?
HARMON. 'Twas I who sold the toy to work the cure.
PRINCE. And honestly I purchased it, I'm sure.

(Assent of Fairies.)

I'm changed from Thomas Tucker, I confess,
But where's Bo-Peep, my beautiful Princess ?
Has Jack in Box betrayed me after all,
Restored my form, and kept the Princess small ?
HARMON. It may be so.   Jack curious tricks will play.
PRINCE. And so, malicious fairy, *that's* your way.

Duet.—PRINCE *and* HARMONICA.

Air.—" Quarrel Duo."—*Madame Angot.*

Ah ! now I see the reason why
That fairy charms are bad to buy.
They very temptingly appear,
But break the promise to the ear.
Oh ! why the story did I trust,
If one could do it that I must.
Well, you have had your Fancy Fair,
And to repeat it never dare.
For I will tell the world without,
What wicked things you are about.
A simple " Thank you !" is your price,
It isn't dear, and very nice.
But when we buy, the purchase is but nought,
And mortal man is then to ruin brought.

Chorus.— *Omnes.*

Oh !   Don't he scold the other,
    What makes him go on so ?
He'll never buy another
    Fairy charm, we know.

HARMONICA. Ah ! now you see the reason why
    Those fairy charms you had to buy.
    Of course they temptingly appear,
    And break the promise to the ear.

Oh! Why the story did you trust,
And think to do it that you must.
Yes, we have had our Fancy Fair,
And to repeat it soon will dare.
Tho' you may tell the world without
What wicked things we are about.
A simple "Thank you!" is our price,
It isn't dear for what is nice.
But when you buy, this lesson should be taught.
You should take care of that which you have bought.

Chorus.— Omnes.

Oh! don't she scold the other,
   What makes her go on so?
He'll never buy another
   Fairy charm, we know.

ELFINA. Cease these disputes, Jack truly worked his spell,
         For here come all the rest restored as well.

(Enter KING and PRINCESS.)

PRINCESS. Good gracious, Tom, do you turn out a Prince?
         I'm greatly changed, and better ever since.
KING. Bless you, my chil——no, that's been said before,
         King of Cockaigne, a crow would suit you more.

(KING gives his own Royal Flourish.)

PRINCE. Jack in the Box, this lesson plainly taught :—
         " Happiness means simplicity of thought.
         Teaching conceit and ignorance are allies,
         And even nursery tales may make us wise."

(Lively dance of characters off. Then stage darkened, and Dark Fairy appears, liberated from captivity by the result of the sympathetic purchase of the Fancy Fair. Testifies her delight by a fantastic dance, at end of which scene changes to

SCENE VIII.

THE GOLDEN LAND OF PLENTY

AND

HARVEST HOME OF THE FAIRIES.

(The FAIRY CORNUCOPIA *advances.*

FAIRY. Here where old Time speeds on with rapid wing,
Welcome to all with every friend you bring.
Plenty we hope to see on every side,
Plenty of mirth these funny folks provide.

HARLEQUINADE COMMENCES.

HARLEQUINS . MESSRS. WILL SIMPSON & WILLIE HARVEY.
COLUMBINES . . MISSES. L. GROSVENOR & S. HARVEY.
HARLEQUINA A LA WATTEAU . . . MISS AMY ROSALIND.
CLOWNS . . . . MESSRS. F. EVANS & W. H. HARVEY.
PANTALOONS . . . MESSRS. PAUL HERRING & J. MORRIS.

TWO HAIRDRESSERS' SHOPS.

Pantomimists—F. Evans, W. H. Harvey, W. Simpson, W. Harvey, Paul
Herring, and J. Morris. Misses Grosvenor, S. Harvey, and A. Rosalind.

A regular **Boxing Match** on Boxing Day—Two Jacks (not fish)—Caught
with a Hook—Clown breaks their hearts, and become regular Young
Shavers.

ENTERTAINMENT BY MR. LEVANTINE, THE AMERICAN WONDER.

Shaving made Easy—General Election, Everybody invited to the Pole—
Clowns do a little Blundering, and of course a little Plundering—
a (n) ice change to

THE ARCTIC REGIONS.

THE NUBIAN SKATERS. THE SISTERS NEVIERS.

FARMYARD, LAUNDRY, AND DAIRY.

Pantomimists—F. Evans, W. Simpson, and J. Morris. Misses Grosvenor and A. Rosalind.

"If I had a donkey wot wouldn't go"—When shall we three meet again?—A Drop in and a Drop out—A Lift over and a Dogmatic Result—Pantaloon framed—the Tale (tail) end of a Joke—on the Roof, a Skylark, a Stily (lish) Affair, and a hard outside brick—Two sheets in the wind, and let go the Painter—Bobby meets with a warm reception, and a painful drop too much—A Kiss and a blunder (buss)—Mistaken Identity—Gone to Walls-end, ending in a Col-lision—Pure Milk and Half-and-Half—A leg up and a cow-hard-ly action—The Iron Cow—Wat-er you at?—Clown takes lea(ve)f-fer another Branch—The Copper in a Copper—Clown sees a Crow—Headifying Result—Skying the Copper—A Force-ible Rise for Bobby—Bobby elevated—Tree-son—Head of the Force Colossal—Which way does the Bull run?—Division of One, and General Division—Daisy Farm, oh?

Acrobatic Entertainment by the BROTHERS ETHAIR.

DOCTOR'S & CARDMAKER'S SHOPS.

Pantomimists—W. H. Harvey, W. Harvey, Paul Herring, and Miss S. Harvey.

Clown has a step that puzzles him, and receives a leg-i-see—Collared Beef versus Cribbage—One for his nob and two for his heels.

PIERO, THE ONE-LEGGED DANCER.

Persian Sherbet—the Great Gun of the Season.

A DANCE OF DOMINOES,

By the Ladies of the Corps de Ballet.

A Game of Cards—Beggar my Neighbour—Honours lost—A regular cut and Shuffle to

INTERIOR OF BREWERY.

Pure Malt and Hops—Morning Arrival to Work, and Evening time to go home.

HOP GROUNDS IN KENT.

HOP GARLAND DANCE.

These Scenes played by One Hundred and Fifty Children.

TERMINATING WITH

ENGLAND IN THE OLDEN TIME!

EVERY MONDAY.

SPORTING OPINION,

ONE PENNY. LC,

CONTAINS

THE CREAM OF THE SPORTING PAPERS

AND

STATISTICAL TABLES.

COMMISSIONS EXECUTED
ON ALL RACES
DURING THE SEASON.

MARKET AND STARTING
PRICES
AS PER DAILY SPORTING PAPERS.

Key Numbers from Shilling Circulars

LATEST BETTING.

SELECTIONS FROM THE PROPHETS.

LONDON :
ROBERT DAVEY, 1, Dorset Street, Fleet Street.

SPORTING OPINION

TURF INVESTMENT AGENCY,

11, DUNDAS STREET, GLASGOW.

ROBERT DAVEY

Begs to announce that, having opened Offices at the above address,
he will, on and after January 6th, 1873, be prepared to

EXECUTE COMMISSIONS

FROM FIVE SHILLINGS TO ANY AMOUNT

ON THE

WATERLOO CUP, LINCOLNSHIRE HANDICAP,
LIVERPOOL GRAND NATIONAL,
CITY AND SUBURBAN,
TWO THOUSAND GUINEAS,

AND

DERBY,

At best Market Prices, lists of which will be published daily, and
forwarded post free on receipt of address.

STARTING PRICE COMMISSIONS

Will also be executed on day of race on

ALL EVENTS DURING THE SEASON,

And prices returned as quoted in the *Sportsman.*

NOTICE!

THE BUSINESS OF

SPORTING OPINION

AND

RACING TELEGRAM PRIVATE ADVICE CIRCULAR

WILL BE CARRIED ON AS USUAL AT

1, DORSET STREET, FLEET STREET, LONDON.

Letters with commissions to be addressed ROBERT DAVEY, 11,
Dundas Street, Glasgow, and P. O. Orders made payable at Glasgow
Post Office. Cheques crossed "City of Glasgow Bank."

T. BOTTOMLEY,

THE OLD ESTABLISHED AND

SUCCESSFUL TURF ADVISER.

Begs to inform his old Subscribers and Sporting Friends that his Subscription List for 1874 is now open, his past unparalleled successes in predicting the winners of all important races are well known throughout the three kingdoms. He is now in a position to advise his Subscribers what to invest on for the following important races:—

Waterloo Cup, Lincolnshire Handicap, Liverpool Grand National Steeplechase, City and Suburban, Great Metropolitan, Northampton Stakes, Newmarket Handicap, Chester Cup, 2,000 Guineas,

DERBY, OAKS,

and all forthcoming events.

2000 to 1 can be obtained against his selections for the double event, "City and Suburban" and "Chester Cup," and 3000 to 1 for the treble event, "Grand National," "City and Suburban," and "Chester Cup." All the horses he advises are sound, well, and intended. Last year he commenced with advising Mornington at 66 to 1 for "City and Suburban," and ended with his old favourite, Sterling, at 20 to 1 for "Liverpool Autumn Cup."

Terms:—Subscription for the whole year 25s.; up to the Derby and Oaks 12s. 6d.; this includes all Key Books, Weekly Circulars, Postage, &c.

ADDRESS:—

THOMAS BOTTOMLEY,

SOMERSET VILLA, EDITH GROVE,
FULHAM ROAD, LONDON, S.W.

Post Office Orders to be made payable at 290, Fulham Road.

LICENSED VICTUALLERS' SCHOOL.
KENNINGTON LANE, LAMBETH, S.

Instituted 1803.   *Enfranchised 1857.*

Patroness—THE QUEEN.

Gentleman's Life Subscription, £10 10s. | **Lady's Life Subscription, £5 5s.**
Annual Subscription .... **£1 1s.**

A Life Subscription of Ten Guineas may be paid by instalments extending over three years.

From the establishment of the Institution up to the present time 1,896 children have been received. Children are eligible for admission between the ages of 7 and 12. Boys remain in the School until 14, and Girls until 15 years of age.

Members of the Incorporated Society contributing £5 5s. to the School, after having belonged to the Society for two years, render their children eligible to be nominated as candidates for election. The neglect of Members to contribute to the School has deprived many children of its benefits. The subscription may be paid by either parent, and prior to the decease of the last surviving parent. Licensed Victuallers not being Members of the Society, on payment of Ten Guineas, either at one time or by instalments, within three years, and subsequently completing two years in business, are entitled to the like privileges.

The annual expenditure for the School exceeds £5,500.

The next Election of Children will take place at the School House, Kennington-Lane, on Tuesday, the 10th of March next. The number to be admitted will be duly announced. No applications will be received after the 31st of December.

GOVERNOR AND COMMITTEE OF MANAGEMENT.
Mr. ROBERT TURNHAM. 234, Euston-road, *Governor.*

Mr. James B. Burgess, 310, Kennington-rd.
Mr. Thomas Potter, 55, New North-road.
Mr. James Towsey, 40, Houndsditch.
Mr. James Bennett, 71, Burton-rd., Brixton.
Mr. James Everson, 13, Upper St. Martin's-lane.
Mr. William W. Peall, 225, Camberwell New-road.
Mr. Joseph Eaton, 214, Kennington Park-rd.
Mr. S. Long, 3, Western-villas, Bath-road, Hounslow.
Mr. Thomas Butt, 25 and 26, King-street, Snow-hill.
Mr. Edward G. Rolls, Albion-road, Stoke Newington.
Mr. John Cairn, 130, Princes-road, Lambeth.
Mr. William Stevens, 2, Wharfdale-road, Caledonian-road.

Mr. German B. Worth, 17, Litchfield-street, Soho.
Mr. W. Godfrey, 41, Spring-gardens, Charing Cross.
Mr. W. Suter, 63, Prince of Wales Road, Kentish-Town.
Mr. Thomas Hayward, 9, London House Yard, St. Paul's.
Mr. Thomas Bartlett, 52, Wilson-street, Finsbury.
Mr. Richard Frost, 48, Gerrard-street, Soho.
Mr. E. J. Dyne, 28 and 29, Stockbridge Terrace, Pimlico.
Mr. John P. Frost, 17, Freeschool-street, Horselydown.
Mr. W. H. Beauchamp, 40, Alma-street, Kentish Town.
Mr. James Merrett, 71, Worship-st., Finsbury.

WILLIAM SMALLEY, *Secretary.*

INCORPORATED SOCIETY OF LICENSED VICTUALLERS.
No. 127, FLEET STREET, LONDON.

Established 8th February, 1794.   *Incorporated 3rd May, 1836.*

Entrance Fee .... £5 5s.

This Society has now been nearly 80 years in existence, during which period upwards of 18,000 Licensed Victuallers have become Members. The present number of Members is about 3,500.

It has distributed more than a Quarter of a Million sterling in weekly allowances, upwards of £100 per week being now received by 312 Members.

Members of the Society, after being in business three years from the date of Membership, if overtaken by distressed circumstances, accompanied by sickness or bodily infirmity, are entitled upon application to the Governor and Committee, and without the necessity of election by the general body of Members, to participate in the benefits of the Society.

Every Child under Twelve years of age of a Member dying distressed is entitled to 2s. per week, and upon the decease of both parents to 4s. per week.

Members are required to take the MORNING ADVERTISER while in business as Licensed Victuallers. One Shilling per annum may be paid in lieu of so doing while out of business.

In a recent Report of the Society it is stated that 48 persons then deceased, who had paid entrance fees of only One Guinea each, received upwards of £18,500, or more than £383 each.

Mr. ROBERT TURNHAM, *Governor,* 234, Euston Road.
WILLIAM SMALLEY, *Secretary.*

LICENSED VICTUALLERS' ASYLUM,

ASYLUM ROAD, OLD KENT ROAD,

SURREY.

Instituted 1827.—Incorporated by Royal Charter, 6 Vic., 1842.

Patron, — **The**

His Royal Highness — **Prince of Wales,**

THE ASYLUM

CONSISTS OF

ONE HUNDRED AND SEVENTY SEPARATE HOUSES,

Chapel, Chaplain's Residence, Board and Court Room, Library, &c.,

And is the most extensive Institution of a Trade character in existence.

ERECTED UPON SIX ACRES OF FREEHOLD LAND.

Every Contributor to the Institution who may afterwards fall into decay, has a right to become a candidate for admission into the Asylum (providing the circumstances of his or her case meet the requirements of the Rules of the Institution), and when elected, to occupy one of the Houses, likewise to participate in the gratuitous supply of Coals, and entitled to a weekly allowance in Money, besides being provided by the Institution with Medical Advice, Medicine, &c.

Many recipients of the Society's bounty have enjoyed a happy home in the Asylum for A QUARTER OF A CENTURY, and received in weekly allowances as large an amount as FOUR HUNDRED AND FIFTY POUNDS.

LIFE DONORS ARE ENTITLED,

For the sum of Five Guineas, and under Ten, to Two Votes at every election of Inmates.

" " Ten Guineas, and Under Twenty, Four Votes do.

" " Twenty Guineas and upwards, Five Votes, do.

Multiplied by Ten, being the average number of vacancies that occur in the Asylum annually.

ANNUAL SUBSCRIBERS.

For One Guinea Annual, One Vote.

And a Vote for every *Additional* Annual Guinea.

Copies of the "Historical Account," showing the Origin, Progress, and Present Position of the Institution, may be had (gratis) at the Secretary's Office.

SUBSCRIPTIONS thankfully received by the Board of Management, the past Officers, Auxiliary Committee, and likewise by

ALFRED L. ANNETT,
Secretary.

67, FLEET STREET, E.C.

CLARKE'S
STANDARD NOVEL LIBRARY.

The Best Works of the Best Authors.

New Editions, post 8vo., price 2s. each; Picture Covers.
Post Free on receipt of Stamps.

ALBERT LUNEL	LORD BROUGHAM.
NO SECURITY	MRS. CHARLES CLARKE.
THE BLACK ANGEL	W. STEPHENS HAYWARD.
THE STAR OF THE SOUTH	Do.
THE FIERY CROSS	Do.
THE REBEL PRIVATEER	Do.
LOVE'S TREASON; OR, THE VENDETTA	
AND THE AVENGER	Do.
OCEAN WAIFS	MAYNE REID.
THE WILD HUNTRESS	Do.
THE WHITE SQUAW AND YELLOW CHIEF	Do.
JACK THURLOW AND I	DR. WM. RUSSELL.
THE HUNTERS' FEAST	MAYNE REID.
THE GUERILLA CHIEF	Do.
LOST LENORE	Do.
THE BOY SLAVES	Do.
THE WHITE GAUNTLET	Do.
THE WOODRANGERS	Do.
THE CLOUD KING	W. STEPHENS HAYWARD.
TOM HOLT'S LOG	Do.
TALES OF THE WILD AND WONDERFUL	Do.
TALES OF LIFE, LOVE, AND ADVENTURE	Do.
RODNEY RAY; OR, LIFE AND ADVENTURES	
OF A SCAPEGRACE	Do.
LORD SCATTERBRAIN	Do.
THE CLIFF CLIMBERS	MAYNE REID.
THE TIGER HUNTER	Do.
THE CORAL REEF	PERCY B. ST. JOHN.
THE GIRAFFE HUNTERS	MAYNE REID.
THE HALF BLOOD	Do.
AFLOAT IN THE FOREST	Do.
KATHLEEN; OR, THE FOUR-LEAVED SHAM-	
ROCK	J. HOLLOWAY.
OUGHTS AND CROSSES	MRS. CHARLES CLARKE.
MUNRO OF FORT MUNRO	Do.

LONDON:

CHARLES HENRY CLARKE, 13, PATERNOSTER ROW,
Sold by all Booksellers, and at all Railway Stations.

THE "LITTLE WANZER" AGAIN TRIUMPHANT.

THE HIGHEST PREMIUMS

AWARDED AT THE

VIENNA EXHIBITION, 1873,

HAVE BEEN GAINED BY

THE "LITTLE WANZER"

SHUTTLE LOCK-STITCH

SEWING MACHINES.

These Machines have been awarded the highest Prize Medals throughout the world wherever they have competed with other Machines, having reached the climax of superiority at Vienna, where, in competition with all the chief English and American Machines, they have been awarded the Two Highest Prize Medals given to any Company or Firm in the Sewing-Machine Trade.

For Prospectus and Particulars apply to

4, GREAT PORTLAND STREET,

LONDON, W.,

OR THEIR BRANCH OFFICE,

EAST STREET, BRIGHTON.

R. SALTER.

SATIN SKIRTS QUILTED TO THE WAIST,
IN ALL COLOURS,

12/9, 14/9, 16/9 to 2 Guineas.   Carriage free.

Costumes in all the New Materials of the Season

6/11, 8/11, 10/9, 12/9, 16/9, 21/-   Carriage free.

May 1st, 1874, we shall commence making our own world-renowned **Registered Batiste Costume** in beautiful colours, with Polonaise, 6/11.   Made to measure at the same price.   Carriage free.

ALL GOODS MANUFACTURED ON THE PREMISES.

R. SALTER,
2, CROMBIE'S ROW, COMMERCIAL ROAD, E.

Tram Cars to and from Aldgate every five minutes.

ENGRAVING ON WOOD.

TO PUBLISHERS.—Wood Engravings for Books.

TO AUTHORS.—Wood Engravings to illustrate the Text.

TO NEWSPAPER PROPRIETORS. — Wood Engravings for Machine Printing.

TO MANUFACTURERS.—Wood Engravings for Catalogues.

TO MACHINISTS.—Wood Engravings of Machinery.

Country Orders executed with care and dispatch.

JOHN SWAIN,
ARTIST & ENGRAVER,
266, STRAND, LONDON, W.C.

JOHN WHITEHOUSE'S SPECTACLES

Are the best. They suit the sight and fit the face. Prices from 2s. 6d. to 21s.

Opera Glasses, in leather cases, from 12s. 6d. Elegant Glasses, mounted in Pearl, Ivory, and Tortoiseshell, suitable for Gifts, Birthday, and Wedding Presents.

MAGIC LANTERNS, WITH BOX OF SLIDES, FROM 6s. 6d. DISSOLVING VIEWS FOR HIRE.

JOHN WHITEHOUSE, PRACTICAL OPTICIAN,

COVENTRY STREET, LONDON, W.

(Near the top of the Haymarket).

THEATRICAL COSTUMES!

SAMUEL MAY, Costumier to Her Majesty's Theatre, Royal Italian Opera, Theatre Royal Drury Lane, Olympic, Lyceum, Haymarket, Strand, Queen's (late St. Martin's Hall), Princess's, St. James's, Sadler's Wells, Britannia, Surrey, Astley's, Royalty, Greenwich, Birmingham, Liverpool, Hull, &c., &c., begs to inform Continental, American, and Colonial Managers, Actors, Operatic Artists, Equestrians, and Pantomimists, that every requisite for the Stage may be had on Sale or Hire at his Repository,

35, BOW STREET, COVENT GARDEN,

And 26, PEMBROKE PLACE, LIVERPOOL.

Portable Theatres for Drawing Room Performances.

THEATRICAL WIGS.

W. CLARKSON, the long-established and principal Maker of Wigs to the most popular *artistes* of the Drama, continues to supply the ladies and gentlemen of the Profession. His many improvements and long practice enable him to supply all manufactured articles belonging to his business of a most complete and perfect construction. Amateurs supplied, and Private Representations attended to, and provided with all requisites for public appearance.

45, WELLINGTON STREET, STRAND.

HOLLOWAY'S OINTMENT

AND PILLS.

GRATIFYING RESULTS. No phase of external ailments can present itself which is irremediable by the early and diligent use of the above remedies.

The merest blotch upon the skin, and the deepest ulcerations of the flesh, yield with the same certainty to the detergent and healing properties of this celebrated Ointment. Bad legs, burns, eruptions of the skin, and scrofulous sores can be cured with facility by the use of this Ointment aided by Holloway's Purifying Pills. Under this treatment the foulest ulcers become clean, and in a few days florid granulations appear, which gradually grow and fill up the cavity with firm and healthy flesh. No drawback or relapse need be feared.

LEWIS'S COLOURED SILKS.

Gros Grains, and Glacés, plain and fancy, from 1s. 4¾d. to 6s. 11d.
Lewis's Black Silks, Gros Grains, from 2s. 11½d. to 10s. 11d.
Glacés from 1s. 9½d. to 4s. 11d.
Lewis's Satins, Colours, from 1s. 4½d. to 3s. 11d.
Blacks from 1s. 11½d. to 6s. 11d.
Whites from 2s. 4½d. to 6s. 11d.
Lewis's Mantle and Costume Velvets.
Blacks from 2s. 11¼d. to 16s. 9d.
Colours from 1s. 11½d. to 7s. 11d.
Lewis's Silk, Satin, and Velvet Stock is the largest and richest in the
Kingdom.

Patterns Free.

S. LEWIS & CO.,

HOLBORN BARS, AND CASTLE STREET, HOLBORN.

THE SUNDAY TIMES,

PRICE, 2d.   PER POST, 2½d.

OFFICE:—NEW BRIDGE STREET, LONDON, E.C.

This Journal has, for upwards of half a century, maintained its character as the leading metropolitan Weekly Newspaper. It circulates very largely among the higher and the commercial classes. It has, on Political, Mercantile, Musical, Theatrical, Sporting, and Artistic subjects, exclusive sources of information of the highest value; and the estimation in which it is held as an Advertising medium, its columns will best attest.

Three Editions are published: the first in time for the Saturday morning mails; the second in the afternoon; and the third at an early hour on Sunday morning—an arrangement the advantages of which advertisers will readily perceive.

Advertisements, to insure insertion in their proper places, should be received not later than Four o'clock on Friday afternoon.

SEEING IS BELIEVING!
ONE PENNY JAR KILLS TWENTY MICE!

MEARING'S
POISONED BAIT.

They eat it readily, tumble over, and die on the spot.

WHEN ONCE USED IS ALWAYS CONTINUED.

A TRIAL SOLICITED.

Sold in One Penny Glass Jars, Hermetically Sealed.

SAMPLES ONE PENNY. OF ALL OILMEN.

HOW'S YOUR POOR FEET?
MEARING'S
FOOT POWDER

A Sovereign Remedy for Tender Feet.

It hardens them, and removes all unpleasantness.

Those who suffer with HOT FEET will find it soothing and refreshing.

DIRECTIONS FOR USE.

Dissolve a part, or a packet, in about three quarts of warm water; let the feet soak well; afterwards rub dry with a towel. To be repeated nightly till tenderness is removed, and then once or twice a week.

See the following selection from hundreds of similar Testimonials:—
Letter 505.—Oldbury, near Birmingham.

DEAR SIR,—I was induced to use your "Foot Powder." Thanks; I can now walk with ease. Yours respectfully, W. CHAMBER.

SOLD BY OILMEN, CHEMISTS, &c.

D

MR. S. GABRIEL,

THE WELL-KNOWN DENTIST,

57, NEW BOND STREET,

LONDON, W.

ARTIFICIAL TEETH guaranteed perfect for Eating, Talking, and Singing.—"They appear to grow from the Gums and are life-like."

LOW CHARGES.

HALF FEES to Servants and others on Mondays and Thursdays.

57, NEW BOND STREET.

HAMILTON'S

PATENT ECCENTRIC LOCK.

The Cheapest and Most Secure Lock in the World.

MAKERS TO THE

ROYAL MINT,

INDIA GOVERNMENT, &c., &c.

SILVER MEDAL

OF THE

SOCIETY OF ARTS.

Locks of all Sizes and Descriptions, Safes, Strong Doors, Cash and Deed Boxes, &c., &c.

Factory:—106, YORK ROAD, LAMBETH.

PILLS (Nos. 1 and 2),

OINTMENT, AND POWDERS.

The Universal Vegetable Medicines.

PREPARED AT THE

UNIVERSITY COLLEGE OF HEALTH, EUSTON ROAD, LONDON,

And Sold by all Chemists and Medicine Vendors.

PAINLESS DENTISTRY.

G. H. JONES, Dr. of DENTAL SURGERY,

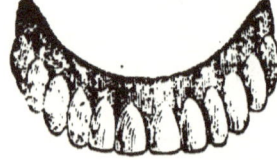

(by Diploma) Maker of every description of Artificial Teeth and Palates, adapts in each particular case the kind most suitable for the Mouth, and is enabled, being the Actual Maker, to supply the very Best Teeth at prices generally paid for the most inferior. Sets from One to Ten Guineas. At home daily, and every information free, at 57, Great Russell Street, opposite the British Museum. Factory, Gilbert Street, Bloomsbury.

TESTIMONIAL.

" My dear Doctor,   Oct. 18. 1873.
            I request you to accept my grateful thanks for your great professional assistance, which enables me to masticate my food, and to add, wherever I go I shall show your professional skill, as I think the public ought to know where such great improvements in Dentistry and mechanical skill can be attained. I am, dear Doctor, yours truly, S. G. Hutchins, By Appointment Surgeon-Dentist to the Queen.—To G. H. Jones, Esq., D.D.S."

THE LONDON FERROTYPE COMPANY,

3a, TOTTENHAM COURT ROAD (near Oxford Street);
2, ALDGATE (opposite Moses & Son's), MINORIES;
32, WESTBOURNE GROVE.

FERROTYPES.

These beautiful Portraits, so popular in the United States, are now being made with great success at the above establishments. They are made on Phœnix-Tinted Iron Plates, are light and portable, may be sent through the Post, or put in Albums, and are

GUARANTEED NOT TO FADE.

From one to eight made at a sitting, finished and delivered in fifteen minutes.
MORNING PREFERRED.

4 FOR 3 SHILLINGS.

D 2

IF YOU BUY YOUR TEAS OF THE

"EAST INDIA TEA COMPANY"

You will require no Medical Analyst, as you may depend on having a pure and unadulterated article.

All Teas in 6 lb. Parcels and 20 lb. Chests, as imported by the Company.

Rich and ripe New Season's Kaisow, at 3s. per lb.

INDIAN TEAS, IN EVERY VARIETY.

WAREHOUSES :—

9, GREAT ST. HELEN'S CHURCHYARD,

BISHOPSGATE, E.C.

ONE OF THE SIGHTS OF LONDON,

CROSBY HALL,

THE ANCIENT CITY PALACE,

BISHOPSGATE,

Two Minutes, from the Bank.

THE GREAT BANQUETING HALL

THE OLD COUNCIL CHAMBER,

AND THE

THRONE ROOM.

FOR LUNCHEONS & DINNERS.

Recherché Dinners at a few minutes' notice.

TOILET ROOM FOR LADIES.

DANCING.

To those who have never learned to Dance.

MR. and MRS. JACQUES WYNMAN and Lady Assistants teach daily all the Fashionable Dances perfectly, to anyone without the slightest previous knowledge. Private Lessons at any time. Schools & Families attended. Highest References. Prospectus on Application. Assemblies every Monday and Thursday at 8 o'clock. A Private Class every Wednesday Evening at 7.30.

Academy: 74, NEWMAN STREET, OXFORD STREET.

Wines AND Spirits.
GUARANTEED ALL FIRST-CLASS ARTICLES.

CHRISTMAS
ENVELOPE CASES,
21/-

Wines AND Spirits.
DELIVERED FREE TO ALL PARTS OF TOWN.

BOTTLES AND CASE INCLUDED, CONTAINING

1 Bottle of	Port	....	Cockburn's.
1	" Sherry	....	Old East India or Pale.
1	" Champagne	....	Moet and Chandon. (First quality.)
1	" Brandy	....	Hennessey's.
1	" Gin	....	Old Tom.
1	" Whisky	....	Irish or Scotch.

A. BEST & CO. (Holborn Wine Cellars),
OPPOSITE CHANCERY LANE.

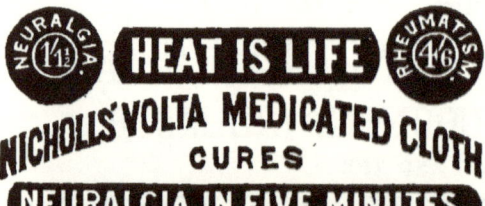

HEAT IS LIFE

NICHOLLS' VOLTA MEDICATED CLOTH
CURES
NEURALGIA IN FIVE MINUTES,
RHEUMATISM & GOUT.
NO MATTER OF HOW LONG STANDING

CURES NEURALGIA
In Five Minutes.
Buy a 1s. 1½d. Box of
NICHOLLS'
VOLTA CLOTH.

RHEUMATISM AND GOUT,
No matter of how long standing.
Buy a 4s. 6d. Box of
NICHOLLS'
VOLTA CLOTH.

Send 15 or 56 Stamps, or P.O.O., to the

Patentee—MR. R. NICHOLLS, 292, HIGH HOLBORN.
Branch Depot, 109, Westbourne Grove.
Or order of your Chemist.

HARRIS-JONES & SHINGLETON,

MERCHANT **TAILORS,**

319, OXFORD STREET,

(Ten Doors West of Regent Circus).

NEWEST & BEST GOODS,

At the Lowest possible Prices for Cash.

THE BEAUFORT PRIVATE HOTEL,

Proprietors, Messrs. DE LA MOTTE.

14 & 15, BEAUFORT BUILDINGS, STRAND, LONDON.

Bed and Breakfast, 3/6 per day.

The best accommodation for Families at moderate charges.
Gentlemen can have their Business or Private Correspondence
Address, and forwarded with safety, and use of Rooms, for Writing,
with Name on Window. TERMS MODERATE.

DANCING,

· IN A FEW EASY LESSONS,

Without any previous knowledge, by

MR. GEORGE GIBBS.

The Valse on an entirely new principle. Private Lessons at any hour.
Prospectus on application.

46, RATHBONE PLACE, OXFORD STREET, W.

SMOKELESS STOVES.

NO FLUES.

NASH & JOYCE'S PATENT PORTABLE STOVES. For drying and warming; require no attention; with one supply of fuel burns twelve hours.

THE NEW REGISTERED PATTERN STOVE for Greenhouses, with ash receiver, may be kept burning all Winter by filling up with fuel every twelve hours, and can be regulated to any required degree. Price 12s. 6d. to 6 guineas. Patent Fuel, 18s. per 120 lbs.; in sacks and bags of 30 lbs. and 60 lbs., at 4s. 6d. and 9s.

AMERICAN CHARCOAL BOX IRON.

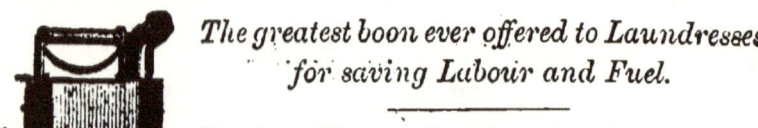

The greatest boon ever offered to Laundresses for saving Labour and Fuel.

Twelve Hours' Ironing for One Penny.

Always bright for use without cleaning. No dust in use, or trouble in lighting. The Iron is a Miniature Portable Stove, with polished surface. Light, Cheap, and Clean. Price, 5s., 6s., and 7s. Prepared Charcoal, 8d. per bag.

PORTABLE VAPOUR AND HOT AIR BATH.
With large Cloak, 21s. and 10s. 6d. Medical Testimonials and Prospectus free on application.

THE NEW PORTABLE STOVE,
For use on the Table. Boils Water and Cooks a Breakfast in a few minutes. Price 7s. 6d. and 10s. 6d. Prospectus.

SWAN NASH, IRONMONGER, 253, Oxford Street,
AND
JOYCE'S STOVE DEPOT, 119, Newgate St., London, E.C.

JAMES GUY,

358, STRAND,

THEATRICAL AND GENERAL

DRAPER & HOSIER

*To the Theatres Royal, Drury Lane, Gaiety, Covent Garden,.
Her Majesty's, Olympic, Adelphi, St. James's, Queen's (late
St. Martin's Hall), Astley's, Surrey, and the principal
. leading Theatres of the United Kingdom.*

A LARGE VARIETY OF

OPERA SILK HOSE,

WHITE AND ALL OTHER COLOURS.

ORDERS & OUTFITS FOR THE COLONIES,

Attended to with Promptitude and Dispatch.

THE ENTERPRISE

LUNCHEON, DINNER, AND SUPPER BAR,

96, LONG ACRE,

CORNER OF HANOVER STREET.

Proprietor - - - - - J. O. HODGSON.

SPECIAL LICENSE.

Visitors to the Theatres and this neighbourhood will find the best Luncheon and Suppers at moderate prices and in great variety at the bar of the above Tavern.

Hot Luncheon daily (Sundays excepted) at One o'clock.

Every Article supplied guaranteed of the Best Quality.

Ales and Stout in Perfection. Wines and Spirits of the Choicest Vintage and Brands.

HAT AND CAP MAKERS,

REYNOLDS, RICHARDS, and Co.,
15, Wellington Street, Strand

(One Door from the Strand),

MANUFACTURERS OF THE CELEBRATED GREASE-PROOF HATS.

D. GOSDEN AND SON,
Contractors

For ADVERTISEMENTS in this and other PUBLICATIONS.

Special Contracts for all Daily and Weekly Papers, Magazines, &c.

Office, 1, CROSS COURT, BOW STREET, W.C.

ESTABLISHED 1837.

PRIZE MEDAL

AWARDED

1862,

W. H. BAILEY & SON,

FOR

LADIES' BELTS.

The increasing demand for these supports has caused W. H. BAILEY & SON to devote particular care to their manufacture. They are made of various qualities and prices to suit all who are suffering from the complaints incidental to females. Sent by post. Prices 15s., 31s. 6d., and 42s.

ELASTIC STOCKINGS

for VARICOSE VEINS. Made of the softest materials in Silk and Cotton; free from any irritation. Prices, 6s. 6d., 10s. 6d., 15s. 6d.; and sent by post for 6d. extra.

A FEMALE IN ATTENDANCE.

IMPROVED INSTRUMENTS

For Spinal and other Deformities.

IMPROVED IMPERCEPTIBLE TRUSSES,

SUSPENSORIES,

ARM SLINGS, CRUTCHES,

RAILWAY CONVENIENCES, &c., &c.

PLEASE NOTE THE ADDRESS:

W. H. BAILEY & SON,

16, OXFORD STREET, LONDON.

(REMOVED FROM 418, OPPOSITE.)

WRITING, BOOK-KEEPING, ETC.,

PERSONS of any age, however bad their writing, may, in eight lessons, acquire permanently an elegant and flowing style of

PENMANSHIP,

Adapted either to Professional Pursuits or Private Correspondence.

ARITHMETIC

On a method requiring only one-third the time usually requisite.

BOOK-KEEPING BY DOUBLE ENTRY.

As practised in the Government, Banking, and Merchants' Offices.

SHORTHAND, &c.

FOR TERMS, ETC., APPLY TO

MR. W. SMART,

At the **INSTITUTION**, 97b, Quadrant, Regent Street,
(Removed from No. 5, Piccadilly).

"A practical, scientific, and really philosophic method."—*Colonial Review.*
"Under Mr. Smart, penmanship has been reduced to a science."—*Polytechnic Journal.*
"A ready and elegant style of penmanship."—*Post Magazine.*
"Calculated to work miracles in penmanship."—*Era.*

"A correct and improved method of instruction."—*Magazine of Sciences.*
"Mr. Smart has great tact in instructing and improving his pupils."—*London Mercantile Journal.*
"Founded on philosophical principles."—*School of Art.*
"We advise all bad writers to apply to Mr. Smart."—*Evening Star.*

*** **CAUTION.**—No connection with any parties teaching in the Provinces or elsewhere assuming the Name, copying the Advertisements, &c., of MR. WILLIAM SMART, whose sole address is

97b, QUADRANT, REGENT STREET.

OBSERVE: PRIVATE AND CARRIAGE ENTRANCE, CORNER OF SWALLOW STREET.

N.B.—Agent to the West of England Fire and Life Insurance Company.

HEAD QUARTERS

FOR

THEATRES, GAMES, AND MAGIC,

2, GARRICK STREET, COVENT GARDEN.

CLARKE'S MINIATURE THEATRES, ready for Acting, with Scenes, Characters, Slides, and Lamps, and a Book of the Play—Price 7,-

ALI BABA ; or, THE FORTY THIEVES—Price 2/6.

BOMBASTES FURIOSO—Price 4/6.

BLACK EYED SUSAN ; or, ALL IN THE DOWNS— Price—5/-

THE WIZARD'S BOX OF MAGIC. Instructions and Apparatus for performing Ten capital Conjuring Tricks sufficient for one hour's Amusement. Post free for 24 stamps.—H. G. CLARKE & CO., 2, Garrick Street, Covent Garden.

THE MOST LAUGHABLE THING ON EARTH. A new Parlour Pastime. 50,000 Comical Transformations. Post free for 14 stamps. Endless amusement for evening parties.—H. G. CLARKE & CO., 2, Garrick Street, Covent Garden.

THE SIBYLLINE MYSTERY (or Magic Cards) reveals to any person, young or old, the object of their choice. Truly Marvellous and surprising. Post free for 13 stamps.—H. G. CLARKE & CO., 2, Garrick Street Covent Garden.

THE MAGIC DONKEYS—Roars of Laughter.—These wonderful Animals go through their extraordinary evolutions daily. The pair sent post free for 14 stamps.—H. G. CLARKE & CO., 2, Garrick Street, Covent Garden.

CUPID'S MAGIC CARDS.—These curious cards will make any person using them reveal their greatest secrets. They defy detection, and cause great amusement. Post free for 14 stamps.

THE ENCHANTED ROSE.—At the word of command a beautiful Rose appears in the button-hole of your coat, and will remain there as long as you please. Post free 13 stamps.

SIR ROGER, THE VANISHING MAN. This funny little figure, on his way to Wagga Wagga, suddenly disappears, and is nowhere to be found. The best Conjuring Trick out. Post free for 20 stamps.

H. G. CLARKE, & CO.,

HEAD QUARTERS FOR GAMES AND MAGIC,

2, GARRICK STREET, COVENT GARDEN.

QUEER FOLK. Fairy Stories. By E. H. KNATCHBULL-HUGESSEN, M.P. With Illustrations by S. E. Waller. Crown 8vo., cloth extra, 5s. Fourth Edition now ready.

YOUNG PRINCE MARIGOLD; and other Fairy Stories. By JOHN FRANCIS MAGUIRE, M.P. With Illustrations by S. E. Waller. Globe 8vo., cloth extra, 4s. 6d. [This day.

SYBIL'S BOOK. By LADY BARKER. Illustrated by S. E. Waller. Globe 8vo., 4s. 6d. [Immediately.

THE CHILDREN'S GARLAND, from the best Poets. Selected and arranged by COVENTRY PATMORE. New Edition, with Illustrations by J. Lawson. Crown 8vo., cloth extra, 6s. [This day.

THE HISTORY OF PRINCE PERRYPETS: a Fairy Tale. By LOUISA KNATCHBULL-HUGESSEN. With 8 Illustrations. New Edition. Crown 4to., gilt, 3s. 6d.

THE FAIRY BOOK. The best Popular Fairy Stories, selected and rendered anew. By the Author of 'John Halifax, Gentleman.' New Edition, with Coloured Illustrations by J. E. Rogers. Crown 8vo., cloth, extra gilt, 6s.

TALES AT TEA-TIME; Fairy Stories. By E. H. KNATCHBULL-HUGESSEN, M.P. Illustrated by W. Brunton. Crown 8vo., cloth gilt, 5s. Fifth Edition.

MOONSHINE: Fairy Stories. By E. H. KNATCHBULL-HUGESSEN, M.P. Illustrated by W. Brunton. Crown 8vo., cloth gilt, 5s. Fifth Edition.

CRACKERS FOR CHRISTMAS: More Stories. By E. H. KNATCHBULL-HUGESSEN, M.P. With Illustrations by Jellicoe and Elwes. Crown 8vo., cloth gilt, 5s. Fifth Edition.

STORIES FOR MY CHILDREN. By E. H. KNATCHBULL-HUGESSEN, M.P. With Illustrations. Crown 8vo., cloth gilt, 5s. Fifth Edition.

MACMILLAN AND CO., LONDON.

THE CHRISTMAS NUMBER OF "GOOD THINGS."

Now Ready at all Booksellers, with 30 Illustrations by Ernest Griset, 6d.

THE GOOD-NATURED BEAR;
BEING THE
CHRISTMAS NUMBER OF "GOOD THINGS."

. "The Good-Natured Bear" is a most striking Story, which will enchant all readers, young and old.

HENRY S. KING & Co., 12, PATERNOSTER ROW.

GEORGE REES,

41, 42, AND 43, RUSSELL STREET,

COVENT GARDEN,

OPPOSITE DRURY LANE THEATRE.

OLEOGRAPHS & ENGRAVINGS.

A selection of the most beautiful Landscapes and Figure Subjects, in handsome Gold Frames, from One Guinea each.

REES'S SPORTING SUBJECTS,

ALL VERY FINELY COLOURED.

FOX HUNTS, 21s. SET. (4).

STEEPLECHASING, 21s. SET (4).

ALL THE DERBY WINNERS, 10s. EACH.

PICTURE FRAME MOULDINGS,

TO THE TRADE AND FOR EXPORTATION,

AT REDUCED PRICES.

GEO. REES,

41, 42 & 43, Russell St., Covent Garden,

Wholesale Depot, 57, DRURY LANE, W.C.

FENDERS AND FIRE-IRONS.

Families furnishing will find it to their advantage to inspect the Stock and compare the prices.

	s. d.		s. d.
Black Fenders	3 6	to	6 0
Bronzed Fenders ..	10 0	,,	30 0
Bright Steel..	65 0	,,	100 0
Bed-room Fire Irons	3 9	,,	7 0
Parlour do.	6 6	,,	10 0
Drawing-room do. ..	11 0	,,	30 0

	s. d.		s. d.
Improved Coal Boxes	6 9	to	25 0
Copper Tea Kettles..	6 6	,,	12 0
Bronzed Tea Urns..	45 0	,,	95 0

KITCHEN SETS, 1st size, 60s. 8d. ;
Medium size, £8 11s. 1d. ; Large size, £24 19s.

Catalogues, with Drawings and Prices of every Article, may be had gratis, or sent post free.

ORDERS ABOVE £2 SENT PER RAIL, CARRIAGE FREE.
RICHARD & JOHN SLACK,
336, STRAND, opposite SOMERSET HOUSE.

KEATING'S

COUGH

LOZENGES.

Known as unquestionably the Safest and Best Remedy for

COUGHS,

ASTHMA,

HOARSENESS,

CONSUMPTION (Incipient),

ACCUMULATION OF PHLEGM,

DIFFICULTY OF BREATHING.

These Lozenges contain no opium nor any deleterious drug, therefore the most delicate can take them with perfect confidence. No remedy is so speedy and certain in its beneficial effects.

Sold by all Chemists, in Boxes, 1s. 1½d., and 2s. 9d. each.

RECOMMENDED

BY THE

MOST EMINENT

OF THE

FACULTY.

Has been awarded THREE GOLD MEDALS for its superiority over all others.

Makes delicious Bread, Plum-puddings, and all kinds of Pastry, light, sweet & digestible.
Sold everywhere in 1d., 2d., and 6d. packets ; and 6d., 1s., 2s. 6d., and 5s. boxes.

FORD'S EUREKA SHIRTS.

41 & 44,   **308,**

POULTRY.   **OXFORD ST.**

FORD'S EUREKAS.
Six for 35s. Illustrations free.

FORD'S EUREKAS.
Six for 45s. Beautifully made, and double-stitched.

FORD'S EUREKA SHIRTS.
Six for 45s. Directions for self-measurement post free.

FORD'S EUREKAS.
Six for 45s. Celebrated for durability and appearance.

ÆGIDIUS.
A new elastic OVER SHIRT, which will entirely dispense with the old-fashioned and ever-shrinking coloured flannel. The Ægidius is perfectly shrinkless, and made from the finest Segovia Wool. Sold by the inventors of the Eureka Shirt.

Patterns of Material and Self-measure free by post from the Sole Makers.

RICHARD FORD AND COMPANY,
41 & 44, POULTRY.
BRANCH:—308, OXFORD STREET.

WILLIAM HOGG'S

Royal Opera Hotel,

OPPOSITE COVENT GARDEN THEATRE,

BOW STREET

(LATE NOAKES'S).

LADIES and GENTLEMEN with CHILDREN visiting the Morning
Performances, will find a very comfortable Coffee Room, and
Luncheons always ready.

EVERY ATTENTION PAID TO SCHOOL PARTIES.

DINNERS from Joint, as usual, 2s.

SUPPERS AFTER THE THEATRES.

GOOD BEDS AND PRIVATE ROOMS.

Public and Private Billiard Rooms.

A PORTER UP ALL NIGHT.

E

BEST FAMILY PAPER.

THE HOME JOURNAL

ONLY ONE PENNY A WEEK.

New Story. By WILKIE COLLINS.

ONLY ONE PENNY A WEEK.

New Story. By EDMUND YATES.

ONLY ONE PENNY A WEEK.

Original Novel. By Miss BRADDON.

HENRY KINGSLEY.	MRS. SOUTHWORTH.
JOSEPH HATTON.	ANNIE THOMAS.
WILLIAM DALTON.	MRS. CRAWSHAY.

All the best Writers in the Home Journal.

ONLY ONE PENNY A WEEK.

" The most popular of all the Weeklies. It deserves success, and has it."
Standard

ONE PENNY WEEKLY.

THE HORNET,

𝔗𝔥𝔢 𝔖𝔞𝔱𝔦𝔯𝔦𝔠𝔞𝔩, 𝔊𝔯𝔦𝔱𝔦𝔠𝔞𝔩, 𝔞𝔫𝔡 𝔥𝔲𝔪𝔬𝔯𝔬𝔲𝔰 𝔓𝔞𝔭𝔢𝔯.

PROFUSELY ILLUSTRATED.

The HORNET contains Special Intelligence and Criticisms upon
Art, Literature, Music, Politics, and the Drama, and is unequalled
in Circulation and Influence in its Specialty.

TWO CARTOONS EVERY WEEK.

The HORNET, post paid, 6s. 6d. per year, in advance. The HOME
JOURNAL and HORNET to the same address, 12s. per year.

Address: STEPHEN FISKE, 147, FLEET ST., E.C.

"Hand me a Torch."—Shakespeare.

HIGH-CLASS POLITICAL, LITERARY, AND FASHIONABLE PAPER.

THE TORCH,

CONDUCTED BY JOSEPH HATTON.

" *The Torch* is full of personal gossip of London life, is chatty, critical, and humorous."—*Bristol Times and Mirror.*

" *The Torch* is to take the place—and more than the place of *Junius.*"—*The Hornet.*

" Mr. Joseph Hatton, the well-known novelist and late editor of the *Gentleman's Magazine,* brings a well-garnished mind and a widely-gathered experience to bear upon this addition to our weekly literature. The tone is high and scholarly, the gossip general and easy, the political writing smart and vigorous. *The Torch* gives an idea of the defunct *Owl,* the *Saturday Review,* and *Pall Mall Gazette.*"—*The Western Mail.*

" *Junius* has been supplanted by *The Torch,* and under Mr. Joseph Hatton's editorship promises to occupy a most important position."—*Sunday Times.*

" Joseph Hatton's idea is to make *The Torch* one of the most brilliant and original publications of its class."—*Exeter Flying Post.*

" Here is *The Torch* to light us on our way."—*Drawing Room Gazette.*

*** Free by post for 10*s.* 6*d.* a Year, paid in advance.

TO ADVERTISERS.

Advertisers who desire that their announcements should come before the Higher Classes should secure positions in THE TORCH. *Only selected Advertisements will be inserted.*

PUBLISHING OFFICE.

147, FLEET STREET.

The Paper can be ordered through any respectable Agent in London and the Provinces.

ST. JAMES'S HALL,
PICCADILLY.

Messrs. MOORE & BURGESS · · Sole Lessees.

The oldest established and most successful Entertainment in the World.

THE MOORE & BURGESS MINSTRELS,

Now in the Ninth Year of one continuous Season at the ST. JAMES'S HALL.

PERFORMANCES
ALL THE YEAR ROUND!

EVERY NIGHT AT 8.

MONDAYS,
WEDNESDAYS,
AND
SATURDAYS.

3 & 8.

THE GREAT COMPANY IS NOW PERMANENTLY INCREASED TO

FORTY-FIVE PERFORMERS!

INCLUDING the FINEST VOCAL CHOIR in the WORLD·

Doors open for the Day Performances at 2.
Doors open for the Night Performances at 7.30.

EVERY WEST-END OMNIBUS RUNS PAST ST JAMES'S HALL.
Passengers by the Metropolitan Railway book to Regent Circus, which is but five minutes walk from the Hall.

COUNTRY VISITORS should bear in mind that the long abused title of Christy Minstrels is totally extinct.

www.ingramcontent.com/pod-product-compliance
Lightning Source LLC
Chambersburg PA
CBHW030027030726
47499CB00008B/3154